PAST TENSE

PAST TENSE

KEN ROBERTS

A Groundwood Book
Douglas & McIntyre
TORONTO/VANCOUVER/BUFFALO

Groundwood Books
Douglas & McIntyre Limited
585 Bloor Street West
Toronto, Ontario M6G 1K5

Canadian Cataloguing in Publication Data

Roberts, Ken, 1946-
Past tense

ISBN 0-88899-214-9

I. Title.

PS8585.02968P3 1994 jC813'.54 C94-931486-2
RZ7.R63Pa 1994

The publisher gratefully acknowledges the assistance of the Ontario Arts Council, the Canada Council and the Ministry of Culture, Tourism and Recreation.

Cover art by Janet Wilson
Design by Michael Solomon
Typesetting by Pixel Graphics Inc
Printed and bound in Canada

This book is dedicated to my parents, although they have not seen each other in many years. Everything I write reflects a respect for people. I learned respect and humour from both parents, not from one or the other.

Writing has always been my late-night hobby — an amusement of sorts. This book has surprised me. It started as another amusement. While it may have amusing moments, it is not a comic novel. It reflects emotions that reside deep in my soul.

Part of this story is based on a true incident, but the incident occurred so long ago that I am not sure what really happened and what my mind has invented.

ONE

AFTER breakfast, I ran down Aunt Lois's wheelchair ramp and slid inside Uncle Chuck's car.

"I've got a friend," said Uncle Chuck in his deep voice, "who makes entire cities out of cardboard toilet-paper tubes. You should see them. They're great. He's building Paris in his basement right now. It should be finished in the spring."

I didn't say anything. I wasn't supposed to say anything. Uncle Chuck wasn't talking to me. He was talking to somebody on his cellular phone. Uncle Chuck did glance at me, to make sure my seatbelt was fastened. I nodded, and he pulled away from the curb.

"You could do a remote shoot from his house," said Uncle Chuck. "Yeah. I'll send pictures. No problem, Stuart. Just remember, I get the finder's fee if you use the idea. Yeah. Standard rate. Bye."

Uncle Chuck hung up and turned to me.

"So, grocery store, right?" he asked.

"Right," I said.

"Your mother give you the list?"

"Of course."

Mom, Denny and I live with Uncle Chuck and Aunt Lois. Uncle Chuck is my father's brother. My father died when I was a baby.

Uncle Chuck and Aunt Lois don't mind us living with them. They need us. Mom organizes their lives, Denny does the cooking, and I listen to Uncle Chuck. He likes to talk. I like to listen.

Uncle Chuck glanced down at his phone and frowned.

"If you want to make a call, it's all right with me," I said. "I don't mind."

I enjoy shopping with Uncle Chuck on Saturday mornings. He's a funny man who is a master at bending the truth. When Uncle Chuck tells Aunt Lois and Mom and Denny what we did, I listen, mouth open, wondering if we've gone to the same places and seen the same things.

Uncle Chuck never tell lies, though. Everything he says actually happened. He just arranges the truth in crazy patterns.

Our shopping trips changed after Uncle Chuck bought his cellular phone. He doesn't talk to me much when we drive, not anymore.

"It's all right?" he asked.

"Sure," I said with a sigh. "It's fine."

Uncle Chuck kept driving, staring down at the phone after checking traffic ahead.

"What's wrong?" I asked.

"Who should I call?"

I laughed.

"Uncle Chuck, you're addicted to that thing!"

He drove, humming to himself. Uncle Chuck hums when he thinks.

"I really am addicted to that phone, aren't I?" he asked at last.

"Yes. Definitely."

"Terrific."

Uncle Chuck picked up the phone and pushed a couple of buttons to dial a number automatically.

"Hello, Stuart?" he said. "I've got another show for you. Here's the pitch. Cellular Phones, The New Addiction. I'm riding in the car and I'm talking on the phone right now. I'm always on the bloody cell phone."

Uncle Chuck pulled to a stop at a red light, turned to me and winked.

My uncle is an independent talk show segment producer. He thinks of different show ideas and then, when the executive producer of a show buys an idea, Uncle Chuck arranges for guests and makes lists of questions for the hosts to ask. Sometimes he has to appear as a guest himself. Most talk shows don't pay guests, but they do pay for ideas, and they pay writers.

Even though Uncle Chuck has been on TV dozens of times, he isn't a celebrity. He doesn't want to be a celebrity. If he had a famous name or a famous face, people would know how frequently he has appeared on the same shows, always with some new and different quirk.

Uncle Chuck is probably the most ordinary-looking person in the world. He isn't tall but he isn't short, either. He wears glasses when he reads. He has brown hair that looks flowing when it's long and thin when it's short. He's a bit pudgy but definitely not fat. Uncle Chuck's real name is Charles Edward Robert Derbin, so when he's on television he has lots of names and faces to use, all of them real.

Uncle Chuck's quirks are all real, too. He was a guest on some Valentine's Day show last year, talking about the life-sized bust of

Aunt Lois's head that he'd carved out of chocolate and given to her. Uncle Chuck didn't carve that head so he could get on a talk show. He carved the head because he thought it would make a great present and then, when Aunt Lois laughed, he realized that he could make a little money by talking about what he'd done. Uncle Chuck is a golden-tongued talker, so TV producers love to book him whenever they can.

"Let me explain something to you, Stuart," said Uncle Chuck as he drove with one hand. "I'm on the way to the supermarket with my nephew, right? Well, I'm going to take this phone into the supermarket with me and make a new call every minute or two, asking Denny or Marta or Lois if they want me to buy the small can of tomato paste or the large can of tomato paste, if they want the Italian bread or the French bread. After the supermarket, Max and I are planning to go to a clothing store downtown where there's a sale. I'll have the cell phone, right? If I see an item somebody might want, I'll call that person and describe it. There are hundreds, probably thousands of people with this same high-tech addiction. Hey, maybe that's the real angle. High-Tech Addictions, from Video Games to Cellular Phones."

There was a pause while Stuart, who books talent onto several talk shows, said something. Uncle Chuck listened and then began to grin. He lifted the hand with which he had been steering and raised it toward me for a High Five congratulations.

Since I wanted to get to the grocery store alive, I smacked Uncle Chuck's hand quickly. He grabbed the steering wheel in time to turn into the supermarket parking lot.

"Sure, Stuart," he said. "The Stan Cardo Show would be great. Talk to Marta, and she'll book a date. I'll find a psychiatrist who can talk about addiction and a person who can talk about how quickly cellular phones are selling." Uncle Chuck started to hang up, glancing at me. "Hey!" he shouted into the phone. "You still there, Stuart? Good. Listen, my nephew Max is riding in the car with me. Marta's been looking for a way to get him in front of the cameras. You know, start him in the family business. Is it all right if I find a spot for him? He could talk about riding around with me doing errands while I constantly talk on the phone. It embarrasses him. What? Nah. It will be genuine. Hey, I'll make sure he's embarrassed."

"That's all right, Uncle Chuck," I whispered.

"He's eleven."

"Thirteen," I said.

"Thirteen, I mean," said Uncle Chuck. "And he's a good-looking kid." Which made me feel good, since Uncle Chuck must have thought it was true. "Dusty brown hair and lots of it. Freckles, even. He'll look great on camera. He can talk, too. Got a great mouth on him. What? He's Marta's kid. Named after his dad, God rest his soul. Maxwell Derbin. We call him Max, of course."

Uncle Chuck listened for a moment and grinned again. He started to lift his hand off the wheel for another High Five but changed his mind since he was turning into a parking space at the same time. I gripped the dashboard and thought maybe Stuart should do a show on the dangers of riding in a car with somebody who uses a car phone. I could be a guest on that show.

"Good. Let's do the show this summer so Max doesn't miss school. His mom will be thrilled. Thanks, Stuart."

Uncle Chuck hung up and eased the car forward, gently nudging a grocery cart out of the way.

"There," he said, pulling on the emergency brake. "Let's go."

"I'm going to be on TV?" I asked slowly. "Me?"

"Sure, kid. It's about time. You'll be great. Just relax and tell the truth. We'll have a terrific time. We'll drive down to Toronto in the afternoon and maybe go to a Blue Jays game and spend the night."

I was nervous. Everybody in my family, except Mom, has been on television. Making a first television appearance in our family is like going to your first hockey practice for some kids. It's something I knew would happen some day. I could hardly wait, but I was still scared.

"Are you really going to take that phone into the store?" I asked.

"Sorry, kid. A deal's a deal. Never let it be said that Chuck Derbin appeared on a talk show and told a lie. If I'm supposed to say I take my phone right into stores, I will take the phone into stores. It may embarrass you. It may even embarrass me, but there's a principle at stake," said Uncle Chuck, pointing one finger toward the ceiling of the car, "and that principle is honesty."

I rolled my eyes.

Until I was ten years old, I loved my family. I loved Uncle Chuck most of all and was glad we lived with him. I still like him, but maybe I see too much of him, particularly during the summer months. Uncle Chuck works at home when he's not taping a show. Too much of a good thing isn't always good. Even too many hot dogs or too much ice cream can make me sick.

Aunt Lois and Mom work at home, too. Aunt Lois writes stories about space creatures for a tabloid newspaper in Montreal, but I don't see her much. She stays in her study a lot.

It's a good thing Aunt Lois writes stories for a newspaper. If she didn't, there wouldn't be a baby picture of me. There are a lot of baby pictures of Denny, but there is only one picture of me.

My dad was the family photographer, and he was sick when I was born. He died over a year later. I guess nobody was thinking about taking pictures.

The only baby picture of me appeared in a newspaper next to a story Aunt Lois wrote. A news photographer took it. I'm wearing a diaper and sitting up and smiling a huge toothless grin. I look pretty normal except for long donkey ears and a nose that looks like a pig snout. I am supposed to be an alien baby found at home plate in Yankee Stadium on Babe Ruth's birthday.

There is a copy of the newspaper photograph taped into one of Aunt Lois's scrapbooks. I think I was a cute baby, but it's hard to tell when the nose and ears aren't mine.

"Uncle Chuck?" I asked as I opened the car door.

"Yeah?"

"Is it true that an alien baby was actually found in Yankee Stadium on Babe Ruth's birthday?"

Uncle Chuck stared at me.

"Have you gone plum loco, boy? That's ridiculous."

"Then isn't Aunt Lois writing lies?" I asked slowly. "That was one of her stories."

"It was?"

"Yeah."

"I'd forgotten," said Uncle Chuck.

It didn't really bother me that Aunt Lois wrote lies. I didn't have Uncle Chuck's fear of lying. I'd told a few myself. But it did bother me that Uncle Chuck was proud of Aunt Lois for writing lies.

"She's not telling lies. She's writing fiction," said Uncle Chuck loudly. "Pure fantasy. Nobody thinks she's trying to tell the truth, so her stuff isn't lies. It's storytelling, like movies and books."

"But there are people who believe those stories," I said quietly.

"Sure," said Uncle Chuck, waving his hand. "And there are people who believe Elvis is alive, too. No logical person believes this stuff. Nobody. It's fiction. The world, Max, is divided into two types of people — those who believe Elvis is still alive and those that accept he is dead. Lois isn't writing for people who think Elvis is alive, and she isn't writing for people who think we are being watched by aliens from another planet. She's writing fantasies for those who don't believe such baloney but like a good chuckle once a week."

"Uncle Chuck?"

"Yeah?"

"You're always dividing the world into two types of people. Aren't there ever three types or four types?"

"Nope. There are only two types, always. There are, however, an infinite number of ways to create two types. There are people who can swim and people who can't swim.

There are people who like to travel and people who don't like to travel. There are people I like and people I detest. Stop asking questions or you'll become one of those people I detest. Let's go. We've got shopping to do! We've got calls to make!"

Uncle Chuck hopped out of his door, grabbing his car phone to take along. I followed, slowly.

TWO

"Broccoli's on sale, Denny," said Uncle Chuck, cellular phone perched against his shoulder as he pushed our grocery cart down an aisle. "I know you usually buy your own ingredients, but the broccoli is cheap. Do you want some?"

Denny is my older brother. He's seventeen. Denny does our cooking. I do the housework and dishes.

Denny likes to cook. Unfortunately, Aunt Lois got him a job writing a cooking column for a local newspaper. Now there is a cycle to Denny's cooking. He writes his column every Friday night. He tries a new dish each Monday night and then, over the next four nights, cooks the same recipe, seeking some subtle improvement in flavour.

The taste may get better each night, but I'm tired of eating the same meal five nights in a row. Besides, it's hard to eat when Denny's always hovering, asking if the newest batch of Tuna Surprise is better than the Tuna Surprise we ate the previous night. Most of the time I think it tastes worse because I'm sick of Tuna Surprise or whatever Denny's trying to improve.

Weekends are different. The rest of us trade cooking meals on weekends. Even though Denny is the best cook in the family, I try to eat as much as I can on the weekends when I don't have to eat the same meal over and over. On weekends, Denny cooks desserts, no meals.

Denny's newspaper column is called "Cooking With Cass," and there's a picture at the top of the column which people are supposed to think is a middle-aged woman named Cass. The editor didn't believe people would try recipes concocted by a teenage boy. The picture isn't a lie, though. It is a picture of Denny, although it doesn't look like Denny. He's wearing a dress, a wig, lots of make-up and women's glasses. Mom's maiden name was Cass and it's Denny's middle name, too, so the name isn't a lie, either.

"Why not? It looks good," said Uncle Chuck.

Uncle Chuck inspected the hunk of broccoli he was holding. I don't know what he expected to find, but he was looking hard.

I tossed a few essentials into the cart. Uncle Chuck and I know our jobs when we shop for groceries. It is my job to make sure we bring home milk and eggs and cheese and bread — all the basics for breakfasts and lunches, which Denny doesn't cook. It is Uncle Chuck's job to make sure we have enough junk food. We are each good at what we do.

Denny buys his ingredients separately. The grocery store gives him a discount in return for a weekly mention in his column. The grocery store owner doesn't know Denny writes the column. He thinks that Denny is Cass's son and that Cass sends Denny shopping for her. The grocery store manager is a middle-aged single man who obviously likes to eat and is always trying to get Denny to introduce him to Cass. He's seen her picture and thinks she's cute. He asked Denny once if Cass was married. Denny said no.

"No broccoli?" said Uncle Chuck to his phone, pushing our cart to one side of the aisle so another cart could pass. "Well, it was worth a try, right? Bye."

Uncle Chuck hung up.

"How are we doing?" he asked as I

checked the unit pricing on different brands of long-grain rice.

"Fine."

"Know anybody with a dog, Max?"

"No," I said, turning to look at Uncle Chuck. It was a strange question, even for him.

"A cat, then?"

"We have two cats, Uncle Chuck," I said softly. "You know that. Hobo and Dibdin. We've had them for years. Hobo likes to sit in your lap at night. Dibdin thinks you're strange and avoids you. Remember?"

"Oh, yeah. Right."

Uncle Chuck started humming. He pressed a button on his phone and then waited while it automatically beeped out a number.

"Hey, Denny, is your mom there? Sure I want to talk with her. Why else would I ask if she was there? Yeah. I'll wait."

Uncle Chuck winked at me. He doesn't wink except when he's waiting for somebody to come to the phone, which means he winks a lot. I'm not sure what those winks are supposed to mean, but I think they mean Uncle Chuck and I are somehow waiting together for the person to come to the phone, which we're not.

"Hey, Marta? It's Chuck. I'm at the store with Max, and there's a sale on cat food. Do we need any for . . . "

"Hobo and Dibdin," I whispered.

"Hobo and Dibdin," said Uncle Chuck. "No? Well, uh, do you know anybody who does need cat food? No? Oh, well, I tried. By the way, Stuart's going to call you. I booked Max and me onto the Stan Cardo Show. I'm supposed to be addicted to cellular phones. Max will be an embarrassed family member. No problem. He will be embarrassed. I'm working on it right now. I'd let you talk to him except I don't think he wants to be seen talking to his mother on a cellular phone in the middle of a supermarket. Right, Max?"

I ignored him.

"He's shaking his head, Marta, pretending to study the cereal boxes like we're not together. There's your answer. He's embarrassed already. Bye."

Uncle Chuck was telling the truth, of course. I was embarrassed.

"Well," he said, pushing the antenna on his phone back into its hidden compartment. "Are we ready to pay for this mess?"

"Sure," I said. "Let's go."

Uncle Chuck grinned at me. He started

pushing the grocery cart toward the front of the supermarket. I trailed behind. Uncle Chuck sort of bounced while he pushed the cart.

"There's a big sale on pet food, in case you have a pet," he mentioned to shoppers we passed. "Broccoli's on sale, too," he added when one shopper smiled back.

There were new editions of the different tabloid newspapers at the check-out counter. Uncle Chuck hardly ever buys magazines, but he always reads them in the check-out line. I didn't mind. Since he was busy reading, he didn't make any calls.

"Hey, Max," he said. "Look. Here's a fascinating article Lois wrote. 'Elvis Portrait Found in Martian Crater.'"

"That will be $87.28," said the cashier.

"Let's buy the magazine," said Uncle Chuck. "The article's a classic. It should go into the scrapbook."

He paid and we left the store.

"Uncle Chuck?" I asked as we pushed the cart across the parking lot toward our car.

"Yeah?"

"You don't believe in telling lies, right?"

"Right. I never tell a lie."

Uncle Chuck unlocked the driver's door

and then reached down to unlatch the trunk so we could put the groceries away. He pulled the newspaper out of the grocery bag and closed the trunk. He held up the newspaper and waved it at me.

"In case we get stopped in a traffic jam or something," he said. He hated to be stuck with nothing to do.

"You never tell lies?" I asked again.

Uncle Chuck opened his door and stood there thinking for a moment. "I haven't told a lie for a long, long time," he said. "And that's the truth."

"But I heard you tell a lie a couple of days ago."

"That's not possible. You've got to be mistaken, Max."

"No. I heard you tell Aunt Lois you weren't going to the movies, but you did go to the movies. I know you did. You told me. You saw *Deadbeats Three*."

I opened my door and sat down in the passenger seat.

Uncle Chuck once appeared on a talk show as a person addicted to movies, and it's true. He sees everything, even rotten low-budget movies. Actually, they're his favourites. Aunt Lois and Mom kid him a lot, so he tries to sneak out of the house when he wants to see a particularly bad one.

Uncle Chuck sat down, too, closing his door. "You're wrong, Max. I never said anything about missing a classic gem like *Deadbeats Three*."

"Yes, you did! I was there! I heard you."

"Ah," said Uncle Chuck. He inserted a key in the ignition, started the engine and flung one arm up onto the back of my seat so he could look for cars. "You are my nephew, although it's not fair to say my favourite nephew since I dearly love Denny as well. Still, you are the nephew with whom I spend the most time. Therefore, I shall reveal a select few secrets about not telling lies." He leaned close to me and whispered, "I have a code of ethics."

"Ethics?" I asked.

"In court, witnesses promise to tell the whole truth and nothing but the truth. My vow of honesty requires me to tell the truth, but only rarely do I volunteer the whole truth. There is an important distinction."

"I don't get it," I said as Uncle Chuck swung the steering wheel and inched through the parking lot.

"The other night Lois, my lovely wife,

asked if I was going to a movie, right?"

"Right."

"Several days after this event you seem to recall that I denied I was planning to go to the movies, right?"

"Right."

He checked for traffic before turning left.

"What I actually said was, 'Do you think I'd go to a movie on a lovely night like this? It's a perfect night for a long stroll.' Think, Max. Do you now recall mention of a beautiful night and a long stroll?"

"Yes," I admitted.

"Please note," said Uncle Chuck as he drove out of the parking lot, "that I never denied planning to see a movie. I merely asked if Lois thought I would go to the movie and then commented that it was a lovely night for a stroll, even though I had no intention of taking a stroll. I walked straight to the theatre and sat in the dark watching *Deadbeats Three*, as you know. I am, Max, a master of misdirection."

We rode in silence while Uncle Chuck beamed. I frowned.

"But isn't it a lie when you purposely try to fool somebody?" I asked.

"I don't think so, no," said Uncle Chuck.

"Haven't you heard of the Noble Lie?"

I shook my head.

"There are times," he said, "when any preacher, any philosopher, any honest and fair person would admit that it is best that a lie be told."

"Like when?" I asked.

"Let's say that a few years from now Denny gets married and his wife has a baby. Let's say it is an ugly baby. I mean really ugly, with a nose like a pig's snout and long donkey ears and . . . "

"You mean like the picture of me when I was a baby?"

"What?"

"The only picture of me, when I was a baby, is from a story Aunt Lois wrote. Some artist gave me a pig's snout and donkey ears."

"Oh, yeah, I remember. Yeah, ugly like that picture of you. You can imagine a baby that ugly, right?"

"Sure. I've seen one. Me."

"Fine. Now, let's say that Denny, being the proud father of this hideous child, doesn't see what the rest of us see — an ugly baby. He sees a cute little cuddly kid. One day, Denny brings the baby to visit you and he puts the tyke in your arms. Denny can't take his adoring eyes off the baby, and he asks, 'So, Max, what do you think? Isn't he cute?' Are you going to say, 'I think that's one heck of an ugly baby you have there, Denny?'"

"No. I wouldn't say that."

"Of course not. You would tell a noble lie. You would say, 'Yes, he sure is cute.' Right?"

"Right."

"So, a noble lie is a lie that is told to save someone's feelings. In movies, when the star's best friend gets shot and is obviously going to die, the hero never says, 'It looks pretty bad, buddy. I think you're going to croak.' No. The hero tells a noble lie."

"You're saying, Uncle Chuck, that people should lie sometimes."

"Yeah. I guess I am saying that, although I never lie. I don't even tell noble lies. If somebody shoves an ugly baby in front of me and asks, 'What do you think?' I say, 'You must be so proud.' All parents are proud, Max. Or, I say, 'Wow! That is some baby!' Notice there is no lie and no hurt feelings. Mind you, not lying without hurting people's feelings is hard work. I've been practising for a long time."

"So, you never lie? I mean, you might lie by accident, right?"

"Never. I'm too careful. Now let's call somebody," he said, changing the subject.

"Who?"

"Who cares?"

We drifted to a stop at a red light. But Uncle Chuck didn't get a chance to make a call. Instead, the phone rang, and he answered it.

THREE

"Max and I will come straight home," Uncle Chuck said slowly. "I know it isn't necessary. I just don't feel like shopping anymore. Is it all right with Ida if we visit this afternoon?"

Uncle Chuck listened for a moment and then said, "Good. We'll see you at home." He slowly placed the phone back in its cradle, took a deep breath and put both hands on the steering wheel.

"What's wrong?" I asked.

"Mr. Cluff came home from the hospital this morning."

Mr. Cluff used to live next door to Uncle Chuck and Dad when they grew up on MacArthur Street. He was their Scout leader and their Sunday School teacher. Mr. Cluff played golf with my grandfather every other Saturday morning, April through October. Uncle Chuck and my dad used to mow Mr. Cluff's lawn in the summer time. When Dad and Uncle Chuck grew up, they visited Mr. Cluff whenever they went back to the old neighbourhood.

"Isn't that good news?" I asked. "I mean, he's home from the hospital." I knew Mr. Cluff had cancer and I knew Uncle Chuck visited him a couple of times a week, after dinner.

"No, Max," Uncle Chuck said quietly. "It isn't good news. Mr. Cluff is home to say goodbye to his wife and friends. The hospital lets terminal patients go home for a few days when there's nothing more they can do."

Uncle Chuck watched the road and didn't say a word. I wanted to make him feel better but couldn't think of anything that sounded comforting.

"I know you liked Mr. Cluff," I said finally.

"Like," said Uncle Chuck firmly. "Not liked. He's still alive and I still like him."

We drove quietly for a few more blocks, me feeling awful about what I'd said and then awful because I was feeling awful when it was Mr. Cluff who was dying.

"I'm sorry," I whispered. "I'm sorry for Mr. Cluff, and I'm sorry you feel bad. I'm sorry I made it sound like Mr. Cluff was already gone."

"You didn't mean it," said Uncle Chuck. "Everybody uses the past tense when somebody's dying. It's as if people want to prove good things happened in that person's life. So they only talk about the past, and they only talk about good times."

Uncle Chuck chuckled softly.

"What's so funny?" I asked.

"I was just thinking about Mr. Cluff and how the two of us, he and I, have a relationship he doesn't even know exists."

"Elspeth?" I asked.

"Yeah, Elspeth."

"Maybe you should go over there and tell him you're Elspeth so he'll know."

Uncle Chuck grinned. "I don't think so," he said. "Definitely not."

Uncle Chuck is a master at making money out of each of his strange habits and hobbies. But he has never tried to sell his strangest quirk of all.

Each year, on Halloween night, Uncle Chuck pulls out a battered suitcase that he keeps in the basement. It's half filled with magic tricks. There's a woman's dress and a wig inside, too, along with make-up and an ancient mint-green overcoat. Uncle Chuck dresses like a woman whom he calls Elspeth, and he drives to a park at the top of MacArthur Street.

Elspeth is a Halloween celebrity now. Every year, hundreds of people wait for her. Flashlights swing past the trees at the edge of the park until one of them catches Elspeth striding toward a log that lies on its side to stop cars from driving on the grass.

Elspeth grins and takes a giant step over the log and onto the paved street. She kneels close to the nearest child, a knight in tinfoil armour or a bum with an eye-liner beard. She pulls a coin from behind a kid's head and holds it up for the crowd to see before dropping it into the child's bag of treats.

The routine is always the same. It's a tradition now. Elspeth clears a circle. She opens her handbag and pulls out three bright-orange balls. The crowd cheers and she begins to juggle, finishing with a toss so high that one ball disappears into the night sky above the streetlight before falling back into view. The ball speeds down toward Elspeth who, almost without moving, catches it and keeps on juggling, barely interrupting her rhythm. The crowd laughs as she bows again.

Every year, after juggling, Elspeth leads the crowd to the first house at the top of the street, the Cluffs' house, and she knocks at the door. Mr. Cluff usually opens it and Elspeth pulls a red silk handkerchief from behind his ear. She waves the handkerchief and then rolls it into a ball. She opens her hands to show that the handkerchief has vanished.

"Trick or treat," she yells, holding out her canvas bag.

Mr. Cluff drops a small present inside. Elspeth bows and steps aside so the crowd can file past the door and get their treats. When the last ghost has been given candy, Mr. Cluff and his wife throw on their coats and lock their door. Mom and I wait for them as Elspeth and her crowd move down the street to another house. Mr. and Mrs. Cluff walk the street with us, house by house, waiting while I collect my candy, too.

Late in the evening, Elspeth stands under a streetlight by a mailbox at the bottom of the street and performs one last trick. She bows and a taxi cab pulls up behind her. Then she quickly hops into the back seat and waves to the crowd as the cab speeds away.

As soon as Elspeth is gone, older kids rush

off to collect treats from other streets. Younger ones ask to be carried, suddenly tired. Mom and I walk back up the street with the Cluffs and have hot chocolate at their house.

I knew we wouldn't have hot chocolate with Mr. Cluff next Halloween. It was three months away, and Mr. Cluff wouldn't live that long.

FOUR

Aunt Lois was waiting for us when we got home. She always waits for us. She likes to help take the groceries inside.

Aunt Lois doesn't have good use of her legs. She can walk a little, with braces and special crutches, but it's hard for her. She had polio when she was young. I know polio caused the problem, but I'm not sure really what that problem is, except her legs are weak.

Aunt Lois's arms are strong, though, super strong. I know, because she wheels her chair everywhere and never seems to be tired.

Aunt Lois would be a nervous pacer if she could pace. Since she can't pace, she rolls herself back and forth across a room when she's thinking. She does a lot of thinking when she writes. There is a permanently worn groove in the living-room carpet. Her study is worse. The carpet grooves look like two railroad tracks with a circle at each end of the room where she has to turn the wheelchair and roll back in the other direction. I suppose, since the grooves are so deep, she doesn't even have to guide the wheelchair anymore. She just keeps it rolling and the wheels turn themselves.

Aunt Lois has gorgeous red hair and a beautiful smile. People stare at her in restaurants. When I was little I used to think they were staring because she uses a wheelchair, but most people don't notice the wheelchair. They stare because Aunt Lois is a person people want to see. It's not just that she's pretty. She laughs a lot and has a huge smile.

One day, I asked Aunt Lois why she had married Uncle Chuck. I remember that the tone in my voice made it sound like I thought she could have done better.

"I love your Uncle Chuck," said Aunt Lois. "He's always telling stories about something that's just happened or something that's going to happen. I married your Uncle Chuck so I'd never be bored."

"It's too bad about Mr. Cluff," Aunt Lois said to me as I pulled open the trunk. "I know your father and Chuck both liked him."

I didn't remind Aunt Lois that Mr. Cluff was still alive. Mr. Cluff was alive but my father wasn't. My father was definitely a part of the past, part of Mom's past, Uncle Chuck's past, Mr. Cluff's past and my past, too, even though I couldn't remember him. He died of cancer when I was seventeen months old.

I handed Aunt Lois a grocery bag.

We always use Aunt Lois's wheelchair as our grocery cart, stacking bags on her lap. When we'd finished, Aunt Lois couldn't see around the mountain of groceries, but it didn't matter. She held onto the groceries, and I pushed the wheelchair up the ramp and into the house. Denny was standing at the blackboard in the kitchen, staring at the list of ingredients for some new dish. Something smelled good.

"We're home," I yelled.

"Shhh!" whispered Denny. "I'm right here."

"Where's Mom?"

"In the garden."

"What's up?" I asked quietly.

"I'm trying to cook. It's important for us all to be quiet."

"You mean like if I say a bad word or

something your food might turn bad?" I asked sarcastically.

Denny didn't laugh. He stared at me. "If you slam a door or jump up and down on the floor or shout," he said, pointing a pot holder at me, "I will twist your arm behind your back and keep twisting until your arm is one millimetre from popping out of its shoulder socket. Is that clear?"

I nodded.

Aunt Lois didn't say anything. She never interferes.

Denny is a defensive tackle on the high-school football team. He lifts a lot of weights, too. His neck is so big it's disappeared. He can carry out any threat he cares to make.

"Why?" I asked.

"I want to be respectful of the food," he said seriously.

"That's ridiculous."

"Hush."

"But we've got groceries to put away."

Dibdin, our oldest cat, walked gently across the kitchen floor, like she knew it was important to be quiet. She hopped out the hole in the screen. Aunt Lois, who fixes most things in the house, has never bothered to fix that screen. It's the perfect cat door.

"I'll put the groceries away," said Denny.

"Fine."

I left Aunt Lois literally holding the bags in the kitchen and walked straight out the back door, shutting it gently.

Mom was gardening. She loves to work in the garden. I like to look at flowers but can only recognize two types — roses and snapdragons. I recognize roses by their thorns, and I recognize snapdragons because when I was little Uncle Chuck showed me how you could make their mouths open and close like puppets. I refer to all other flowers by colour and size. "Hey, I like that short gold flower," I might say. Mom always answers by reminding me that the short gold flower is actually called a Bellzebubbulum, which is probably not the real name for any short gold flower, since I just made it up.

"Hi, Mom."

"Oh!" she said loudly, standing up fast. She turned, saw me and took a deep breath.

"Scared you, eh?" I asked.

"Yes, you did."

"Sorry."

"That's all right. I was daydreaming. I hear you're going to be on television."

"Yeah."

"You'll do fine," said Mom, smiling to let me know there was no pressure. She knelt again and began to dig in her garden. She was transplanting some flowers from a box.

My mom is the smallest adult I know. I was the first kid at school to be taller than my mother. I was taller than Mom in the fourth grade. I beat everyone else by at least a grade. Some kids said it wasn't fair since I wasn't even a tall fifth-grade kid, but it isn't my fault I have a short mother.

Mom buys most of her clothes in the children's section where things are cheaper. She likes the styles, as long as the clothes don't have cutesy logos.

"Mom?" I asked.

"Yeah?" she said.

"You heard about Mr. Cluff?"

Mom stopped and put down her digging tool. She stood and looked up at me.

"Yes. Aunt Lois told me. She took the call."

"Are you going this afternoon, too?"

"We're all going."

"What do we say to him?" I asked. "I don't know what to say to a person who's going to die."

I could feel my heart beat faster. I hadn't known I was going to ask Mom what to say, but when I did, it felt like such an important question.

"I don't know, my sweet young son," said Mom. "I never have," she added quietly, probably thinking about Dad.

Mom calls me her sweet young son because I made her love chocolates. Mom loved chocolates when she was growing up but then, when Denny was born, she couldn't stand them anymore. Having Denny seemed to knock her chocolate taste bud loose. When I was born, she suddenly liked chocolates again.

"I suppose," she said, "we should do what we do every time we see Mr. Cluff. We ask about the bridge."

Mom didn't meet the Cluffs until after Dad and Uncle Chuck had grown up and left the house on MacArthur Street. The Cluffs came to my parents' wedding and they came to my father's funeral. Mom didn't see them much, except on Halloween night when we stopped for hot chocolate.

"How's the bridge coming?" Mom asked Mr. Cluff every year, as soon as he stepped out of his kitchen with the hot chocolate.

Mr. Cluff was tall and thin, although his

wife said that he was even skinnier when she met him in high school. Some years he had a moustache and some years he didn't. Each year, though, he had less and less hair on top of his head.

Mr. Cluff had been building a bridge the entire time Uncle Chuck and Dad lived next door, which was sixteen years, and he'd been building it ever since they moved away.

When he was a boy, Mr. Cluff wanted to design bridges. He didn't have the money to go to university, though, so he worked for his father and then set up a business of his own. He sold pots and pans to restaurants.

The bridge Mr. Cluff was building existed in his head.

"The bridge is fine," said Mr. Cluff every year, bending so Mom could take her drink from the serving tray.

"I don't believe there is a bridge," Mom said, sipping her hot chocolate. "Have you got anything on paper? Drawings, plans, anything?"

"Nope," said Mr. Cluff, grinning. He sat down, blew on his hot chocolate and prepared for the routine.

"Then how can you prove this bridge exists?" Mom asked.

"I can't," said Mr. Cluff. "And I don't need to prove it exists. I'm not building this bridge for you. I'm building it for myself."

"If that bridge is not inside Tim's head," said Mrs. Cluff, "he's been pulling a pretty elaborate joke. Every summer we have to drive up to Bala, in the Muskokas. The bridge is designed to span the gap between Bala and a cottage we rent near the Queen's Walk. We stay at the cottage and Tim takes soil samples and tests wind conditions."

"That doesn't prove he's building a bridge," said Mom. "It just proves he likes to vacation in the Muskokas and is willing to poke around a beach for a couple of weeks each year to convince people he's building some imaginary bridge."

"What about the books?" asked Mr. Cluff. "Our basement is full of books on engineering and bridge building. Why would I buy and read all those books if I wasn't building a bridge?"

"Chuck reads murder mysteries," said Mom, "but I don't see him killing people."

"I am building a bridge," said Mr. Cluff with a grin, "and it's all in here," he added, pointing at his head. "It's a beautiful suspension bridge, taller than the Golden Gate. And

I'm going to name it after my wife."

Mrs. Cluff stood up and walked over to her husband. "Can I cut the ribbon?" she asked, pretending to slice the front of her husband's head.

Mr. Cluff laughed. "Listen," he said, grabbing his wife and pulling her down onto the chair with him. "I don't care if any of you believe me. I drive a lot, and I don't like the radio. This bridge keeps me sane."

"Sane!" yelled Mrs. Cluff. "Building a complete bridge in your head, bolt by bolt, is sane?"

"Hey, we're all a little crazy inside," said Mr. Cluff, sipping his hot chocolate. "I just admit what's going on in my head. I'm proud of my bridge. It's coming along nicely," he said every year.

"Mom?" I asked.

Mom pulled off her gardening gloves and stared at me. The sun was behind me. She had to squint and shade her eyes with one arm.

"Last Halloween, just before he went into the hospital, Mr. Cluff mentioned that it was going to take him another couple of years to finish his bridge, right?"

"I remember," she said. "You're wondering if he'll ever finish?"

"Yeah. I suppose."

"He's pretty weak, Max, and he may not be thinking too clearly. Besides, he has a lot of other things on his mind. No. I can't imagine he'll ever finish that bridge."

"So the bridge will cease to exist. Poof."

"Cease to exist? You figure that bridge exists now, even though it's only in Mr. Cluff's head?"

"Yeah. Don't you?"

Mom thought for a moment.

"Sure," she said. "It exists."

"He's worked so hard, Mom. It doesn't seem right."

Mom dropped her gloves into a wooden box that held her gardening tools.

"Did you know that your father spoke perfect French?" she asked.

"He did?"

"Yeah. I knew him in high school, you know, and he took French and learned it easily. It was amazing. Mind you, he never had to use it much. But when we'd run into somebody who did speak French, your father could carry on a perfect conversation. I used to say it was proof of a past existence. When your dad died, I remember thinking it tragic that one person could know so much and then, suddenly, all that knowledge was gone. I knew death meant that your dad with all his warmth and humour was gone, but somehow it seemed wrong that his knowledge could disappear, too."

"Did Dad have the same kind of cancer as Mr. Cluff?"

"No."

"Do you miss him?"

Mom breathed deeply. She reached out for me and gave me a hug. I didn't resist.

"Every day, my sweet young son. I miss him when you do something funny or when Denny cooks an especially good meal. Every day, when I see you or Denny do something, even something ordinary like the way you sometimes walk with one arm swinging more than the other, just like your dad swung his arm, I miss him so much because I know he loved you. I miss having that love around the house. I miss sharing you with somebody else. Chuck and Lois are terrific, but there is something special about the unconditional love for your own child that is part of being a parent. I feel sorry for people who have children and then divorce. If they don't like each other, then they can't talk with each other about their children. I miss telling your dad about things you and Denny have done. Listen," she said, letting go of me and avoiding my eyes, "I've got to get back to my garden."

I didn't say anything. I watched Mom dig in the dirt for a moment and then turned back toward the house.

I'll bet she does miss Dad. I miss him, and I never knew him, not really.

FIVE

I slammed the door.

"Damn it, Max," shouted Denny. "My cooking, remember?"

"Oh, yeah. Forgot. Sorry. What are you cooking, anyway?"

"Pies."

"Pies?"

"Yeah. What's wrong with cooking pies?"

"Nothing. I just never knew you had to talk and walk slowly when pies were cooking. I thought they were pretty sturdy."

"It's part of my new theory," said Denny. "People talk to their plants to make them grow, right? I figure," he said seriously, "that maybe food will taste better if we're all a little respectful while the cooking's taking place. It's an experiment. If it works, I'll write a column for the newspaper. Maybe even a book."

"Denny, the vegetables and fruits have all been cut and picked and pulled out and sliced. I don't think plants want to hear baby talk when they're being tortured."

Denny rolled his eyes.

"You're nuts!" I muttered as I walked out of the kitchen.

Aunt Lois was in her study, just off the living room. There isn't a regular door to Aunt Lois's study. There's a wide opening. Her study used to be a dining area, but we eat in the kitchen. She was working on a story, staring at her computer screen and typing quickly.

I didn't say anything. Aunt Lois doesn't like to be disturbed when she's pressing keys. If she's sitting there, staring at the ceiling, she doesn't mind.

I looked back toward the kitchen. The door to the basement was open, which was unusual. I quietly walked over to it and went downstairs.

There is a laundry room at the bottom of the basement stairs. The laundry room has an acoustic tile ceiling, a painted concrete floor and fake wood panel walls.

At the end of the laundry room there is a door, and through the door is a big room with our old upstairs carpet spread on the floor and a ping-pong table in the middle.

Half the ping-pong table is piled with boxes of clothes. The other half is piled with tools.

Whenever something needs to be fixed, Aunt Lois sends Mom or Uncle Chuck downstairs for the right tool. She can stand and walk a little, but she has a hard time with stairs. If she can't reach whatever has to be fixed, she supervises. If the problem's in the basement, she sits in the kitchen and sends Mom or Uncle Chuck to inspect and shout up the stairs, telling her what's wrong. She drinks coffee and gives instructions, like a pilot in a control tower guiding some non-pilot to a safe landing.

When I was about seven years old, Uncle Chuck used to disappear into the basement to practise his magic tricks. He only performs magic tricks on Halloween night, as Elspeth, but he practises all year. Since I wasn't supposed to know he was Elspeth, I wasn't allowed to go down to the basement when he was practising.

Sometimes, after I'd been put to bed, a taxi would drive up and a strange man would get out. My bedroom faces the front of the house and when I heard the car pull up, I'd get up and peek out the window. There was never enough light to see the face of the man who was visiting, but I knew it was always the same man and I knew it was a man I never saw except late at night.

Uncle Chuck always answered the door and took the man down to the basement. I learned, years later, that the man was Mr. Singh, a wonderful magician who also worked as a taxi driver. He helped Uncle Chuck with his tricks, and he drove the taxi that waited for Elspeth at the bottom of MacArthur Street every Halloween.

When I was about nine years old, I decided that Uncle Chuck was a secret agent. I must have just seen an action movie. I didn't think he was a secret agent for the bad guys. I thought he was on our side but couldn't say anything because all his cases were top secret.

The next time Mr. Singh visited, I sneaked down the basement stairs. I stood in the laundry room and tried to listen through the door. Uncle Chuck and Mr. Singh were talking about hidden compartments and how to make sure some type of box could be inspected without the compartment being found. I heard enough to know that what they were saying could only be secret-agent talk.

The next day, at breakfast, I waited until

Denny had left to get dressed and Mom and Aunt Lois were out of the room. Uncle Chuck likes to linger with a second cup of coffee while he reads the newspaper. As soon as we were alone, I asked him if I could see his gun.

Uncle Chuck looked up at me, equally stunned at the question and at my daring to talk to him during breakfast. He doesn't like to be disturbed when he's reading the paper.

"What gun?" he asked.

"The gun you use at work," I said, wiggling my eyebrows in what I hoped was a clear signal that I knew all about the fact that he was a secret agent.

"At work?"

"Yeah. At work," I said uneasily. I had always wanted Uncle Chuck to pay attention to me. Now he was paying attention. His eyes were narrow and staring hard.

"Why would I need a gun?" he asked.

"You know," I said, wiggling my eyebrows even more.

"I know what?"

"Secret compartments. Secret stuff. You know."

I figured Uncle Chuck was either an extremely good secret agent who had been taught never to reveal his identity, or I was heading for trouble.

"Where did you hear about secret compartments?" he asked.

For a short moment I wondered if maybe Uncle Chuck was a secret agent for the bad guys, and I was in deep trouble.

"I . . . I listened at the basement door last night."

Uncle Chuck laughed. He laughed so hard that his face pointed up toward the ceiling and all I could see was his Adam's apple bobbing up and down.

Mom poked her head in the kitchen door.

"What's so funny?" she asked.

"Nothing much," said Uncle Chuck. "Want to hear a joke?"

Since Uncle Chuck had been laughing, Mom assumed I had just told a joke, but Uncle Chuck didn't say I'd told a joke. He didn't lie.

"Sure," said Mom.

"Let me tell, all right?" said Uncle Chuck, looking at me.

I nodded, of course.

"Two horses are running along together. One horse turns to the other one and says, 'I can't remember your name but your pace is familiar.'"

Uncle Chuck laughed again, showing his Adam's apple.

Mom frowned.

"It's not funny," she said, walking back out of the room.

Uncle Chuck stopped laughing. "It isn't funny, is it?" he asked, taking a bite of corn flakes.

"No," I said.

"Sorry. It was the only joke I could think of so fast. Scary, isn't it? Uncle Chuck shivered and then looked at me. "So," he said, "you think I'm a secret agent?"

If Uncle Chuck could fool Mom, he could fool me. A person who can fool people would make a good secret agent.

"Yes," I said, staring him in the eyes. "I think you are a secret agent."

"Would you like to come to the basement with me the next time Mr. Singh visits?" asked Uncle Chuck.

"Mr. Singh? The man who comes at night sometimes?"

"The man who comes to visit me. His name is Mr. Singh. Do you want to meet him?"

"I can meet him?"

"Sure."

"Is he your contact?" I whispered.

"My teacher," said Uncle Chuck mysteriously. He looked around to make sure nobody else was listening and then leaned close to me. "He taught me everything."

"Sure," I said slowly, not at all sure I wanted to meet Mr. Singh.

"Fine," said Uncle Chuck.

He picked up his newspaper and started reading again.

Mr. Singh didn't visit our house for another two weeks and three days. Every night, I listened for his car. Every night, just before falling asleep, I wondered whether Uncle Chuck would wake me up and take me to the basement. Every night, I imagined a different reason for their secret meetings. By the time Mr. Singh did drive up to the front of our house, I was convinced that he and Uncle Chuck were bank robbers about to initiate me into their gang. I would try to reform them, of course. I practised the arguments I would use.

I was in my room studying when Mr. Singh's car stopped in front of the house. I knew it was him. I heard him knock at the front door and heard Uncle Chuck open the door. I heard a muttered conversation, then Uncle Chuck walking down the hall.

He opened my door.

"Mr. Singh's here," he said gently. "Are you coming?"

I nodded and followed Uncle Chuck to the basement.

Mr. Singh was waiting for us, standing beside a cleared section of the ping-pong table.

"Mr. Singh," said Uncle Chuck. "I would like for you to meet, formally, my nephew Max."

Mr. Singh held out his hand and I shook it. He was grinning at me. He had a wide grin. Mr. Singh was the first man I'd ever met who wore a turban. He was older than I'd thought, glancing at him from my room so many evenings.

"What we are about to tell you is top secret," said Uncle Chuck seriously. "It cannot be told to anyone, except to your mother, to Aunt Lois and to Denny. They know. They are the only ones who do know, however. You cannot tell your best friends, your worst enemies or your teachers. Is that clear?"

The biggest secret I had ever been asked to keep was the fact that Uncle Chuck had purchased a new computer for Aunt Lois one Christmas. I didn't keep it, either. I told.

"I don't know if I can," I said slowly.

"Then you must leave," said Uncle Chuck. "The secret is too important."

"I have to know," I said, panicked. "Don't make me leave. I can keep the secret. I can."

Uncle Chuck glared at me. He looked at Mr. Singh, who was staring at me, too. Mr. Singh turned to Uncle Chuck and nodded.

"He can be trusted," said Mr. Singh.

"Sit down," Uncle Chuck said to me.

I sat in a lawn chair with a wobbly leg. Uncle Chuck reached under the ping-pong table and picked up an old suitcase I had seen but never touched, knowing somehow that I shouldn't. Uncle Chuck walked into the laundry room and closed the door behind him. I sat, trying not to look at Mr. Singh. He stood in a corner, half hidden in the shadows. I stood up and waited beside the table.

I heard the old suitcase open in the other room and heard rustling noises and sounds. After several minutes, the door opened.

Elspeth stood in the laundry room. The bare lightbulb from the ceiling gave her a halo and put her face in shadow.

I jumped, surprised.

"It's me," said the woman. Our cat, Hobo, rubbed against Elspeth's leg and purred. I shivered and looked at her again.

"You're Elspeth," I said, shocked and disappointed. I had always loved Elspeth but certainly never wanted her to be related to me. Elspeth was a clown.

"Yes," said Uncle Chuck.

"But why?"

"It started years ago," Uncle Chuck said, stepping into the room. "Your dad and I were too old for Halloween. We helped Mom hand out candy one year, and I guess we handed out fistfuls because we ran out. Mom got mad and told us to do something, fast. It was your dad's idea to dress up in some of Mom's clothes and walk up and down the street, collecting candy. We did it, putting on lots of make-up so nobody would recognize us. It was fun. We did it the next year, too, adding a few tricks. We did it every year, even after we grew up. When your father died, I kept going back."

"And Mr. Singh?" I asked.

"I met Ahmed at a magic conference," said Uncle Chuck. "He's my coach."

"And I drive the taxi," said Mr. Singh.

I had no trouble keeping Uncle Chuck's

secret. I was old enough to know it was embarrassing to have an uncle who dressed up like a woman on Halloween night, even if he did entertain people.

I walked across the laundry room and opened the door.

Uncle Chuck was standing at the ping-pong table, Elspeth's suitcase open in front of him. I wasn't surprised that he would practise magic tricks after hearing about Mr. Cluff coming home. He practises when he wants to be by himself. He hums while he practises. Uncle Chuck says that my dad and my grandfather and my grandmother all hummed or sang while they worked and when they thought. "Heck," Uncle Chuck liked to say when people commented on his humming. "Even our sewing machine is a Singer."

Uncle Chuck looked up, surprised.

"Sorry," I said and started to close the door,

"Tell me if this trick works," said Uncle Chuck.

He spread a green felt cloth on the ping-pong table and placed three red sponge balls on top.

"Pick one," he said.

I pointed to the ball in the middle.

Uncle Chuck picked up the middle sponge ball, pinching a little bit of it between his thumb and finger, waving the ball in front of me.

"Open your hand," he said.

I held out my hand and Uncle Chuck placed the sponge ball on my palm, closing my hand.

"Can you feel that sponge ball inside your fist?" he asked.

I nodded.

"Good. Now, I am going to try to steal that sponge ball out of your hand without you seeing anything."

I gripped the sponge ball tightly.

"This trick works by magnetism," said Uncle Chuck.

He picked up one of the other sponge balls and placed it in the palm of his hand. He closed his hand. He touched the top of my closed fist with his free hand, and I tightened my grip even more. Uncle Chuck touched his closed palm, muttering to himself.

"*Voilà!*" he said, opening his hand.

There was nothing in it — not the sponge ball I had seen him place in his palm and certainly not the one I could still feel inside my hand.

Uncle Chuck stared at his hand for a moment and then turned toward me, confused.

"Open your hand," he said. "I want to take a peek."

I opened my hand. I was holding two sponge balls.

"Aha," said Uncle Chuck. "I got it backwards."

For the next five minutes, sponge balls seemed to be everywhere. It was an impressive trick.

"That's terrific," I said when Uncle Chuck had finished. I didn't ask how it worked. The solutions are always so disappointingly simple.

There are different types of magic tricks. There are box tricks, complete with trap doors and mirrors and written instructions. There are card tricks which require no skill other than an ability to count. There are also sleight-of-hand tricks which fool the eye, like the sponge balls. Uncle Chuck's tricks require practice and a flair for the dramatic.

"How did you become so good?" I asked.

"Easy," said Uncle Chuck. "I don't like to watch magic."

"You don't?"

"Nope. Most magicians are people who

are easily fooled, which is why they love magic. They are people who are so entertained by the art of magic that they want to learn tricks. But they're not necessarily good magicians. I am a good magician because I'm not easily fooled. I started learning magic because Elspeth needed to do more than ask for treats. Give me a crowd, and I'll do anything to amuse them, even learn magic."

Uncle Chuck held out a card, quickly rotated his wrist, and the card vanished. "Most magicians," he said, "do twenty tricks in a show, rapidly hopping from dancing canes to vanishing doves. A good magician does maybe five tricks in an entire show, but each trick is carefully designed to make the audience have fun. Good magicians know more than how to perform tricks. They know how to entertain."

"I think Elspeth is a good magician, then," I said.

Uncle Chuck laughed. "You may be right," he said, closing his suitcase. "When I put on that outfit, I'm a different person. There is a light in my eyes. I can feel it. I may not like magic, but Elspeth loves it."

Uncle Chuck hoisted the suitcase off the table and headed toward the door leading to the stairs. The suitcase never left our basement except on Halloween night. It only left the basement when Uncle Chuck was heading for the park above MacArthur street so he could become Elspeth.

"What are you doing?" I asked, surprised that Uncle Chuck was taking Elspeth's suitcase out of the basement on a summer afternoon. "Where are you going?"

"Elspeth has to make a visit," said Uncle Chuck calmly. "She's going to see Mr. Cluff."

SIX

I like Elspeth. I liked her when I was small because she did magic tricks. I liked her when I was older because she stayed in another neighbourhood, and nobody knew she was related to me. I did not like the idea of Uncle Chuck packing up his tricks and his wig to entertain a man who had just come home from the hospital to say goodbye forever to his wife and friends.

I ran up the stairs, chasing Uncle Chuck.

He was already outside, walking toward the car. I ran through the kitchen, slamming the door behind me. Denny screamed, but I didn't care.

Uncle Chuck was putting Elspeth's suitcase into the trunk.

"You can't dress up and go do magic tricks for a person who's dying," I yelled. "Are you nuts?"

Uncle Chuck closed the lid and opened the driver's door.

"You coming?" he asked casually.

"No!"

"Goodbye, then."

I jumped into the passenger's side.

Uncle Chuck sat down and buckled his seatbelt. I buckled mine, too, and he started the car.

"This is crazy, Uncle Chuck," I said.

Uncle Chuck didn't say anything. He backed out of the drive and headed toward the park above MacArthur Street.

"Aren't you going to talk to me?" I asked. "Please talk. Please. This is serious. You can't do this, Uncle Chuck. Mr. Cluff is dying and you're planning some sort of practical joke. Listen, please. You are an extremely creative person, but maybe, just maybe, you should consider the fact that creative people aren't always sensible when it comes to — "

"Who says creative people aren't sensible? That's hogwash."

"Everybody knows that creative people are dreamers and dreamers aren't realistic. You're proving that right now. You are driving to the home of a dying man so you can put on a costume and do magic tricks. That's wrong, Uncle Chuck. You can't make a coin appear from behind Mr. Cluff's ear and then pretend you've done something wonderful! Mr. Cluff is dying!"

The phone rang, and Uncle Chuck picked it up.

"Hello," he said. "Yeah, Marta. Max is right here. He's with me. He's fine. Just a second."

Uncle Chuck pulled the phone away from his ear and glanced at me. "It's your mother," he said calmly. "Denny told her we ran from the house and sped away. Denny told her we were mad at each other."

"No, Marta," he said "We're not fighting. Everything is fine."

Since Uncle Chuck never lied, he really did think everything was fine. I didn't.

"Yes," he said, "we were arguing. We're still arguing," he added with a short laugh. "Or at least Max is arguing. I'm just listening. Last I heard, he thought I was an insensitive daydreamer who needed a lesson in the real world. I don't think he's used the term *real world* yet, but he's probably planning to use it as soon as I hang up."

I had been planning to say something about the real world.

"Marta," said Uncle Chuck. "I'd love to talk. After all, the longer we talk, the less

Max can yell at me. But I think I'd better hang up and take my medicine. We'll be home in about an hour."

He hung up.

"Why didn't you tell her where we're going?" I asked.

"Simple," said Uncle Chuck. "Marta would agree with you."

"There!" I yelled. "Mom is one of the most *sensitive* people in the world. Doesn't that make you wonder if maybe, just maybe, you are wrong? What will happen if Mr. Cluff or maybe Mrs. Cluff doesn't want to see a magician right now? Imagine interrupting one of their last days together. They might be sitting on the couch looking through photo albums, remembering good times and holding each other. Suddenly, there is a knock at the door and this clown is standing there, wanting to do magic tricks. Uncle Chuck, I am begging you. Do not do this."

"And I am telling you, Max, that I am going to see Mr. Cluff, whom I have known almost my entire life."

"But you're not going as yourself!"

"Trust me, Max. Trust me."

Uncle Chuck pulled into the parking lot of

the park behind MacArthur Street and stopped in front of the washrooms. A few kids were racing their bikes around the base path at one baseball diamond. A little league practice session filled the other diamond. Some older kids were playing lacrosse at the outdoor hockey rink.

"You can't walk into that washroom and put on a dress, Uncle Chuck! Somebody will see you!"

"I'll dress in a stall," he said, releasing the trunk latch as he hopped out of the car.

"But you'll have to walk across the park as Elspeth. People will notice."

"They won't notice. It's summer. Elspeth doesn't need her coat. People are used to seeing her in a coat. They'll just see a woman walking across the park. It happens all the time, you know."

"They'll see you coming out of the stall or out of the men's washroom. They're going to think you're strange, Uncle Chuck. You could get hurt."

"Stand guard, then. Tell me when it's safe to come out."

"I'm not going to help you, Uncle Chuck! I'm not!"

Uncle Chuck lifted Elspeth's suitcase from

the trunk. He closed the trunk and walked around the car to my door. He leaned down and smiled at me.

"If the phone rings," he said calmly. "Don't answer."

Uncle Chuck picked up his suitcase and walked into the washroom. I sat still for a moment and then hopped out of the car, locked it and nervously walked toward the hockey rink. I sat in the stands where I could watch the washroom door.

The lacrosse players took a break. Three of them shared a warm drink. Another pulled open a knapsack and retrieved a candy bar. Two players sauntered toward the washroom and disappeared inside.

I gripped the bench tightly and stared at the washroom door. I waited a few more moments and then leaped from the bench and ran toward the washroom, afraid of what those lacrosse players might think if they found a man dressing up in women's clothes.

The two teenagers were washing their hands, laughing and talking about the game. They didn't pay attention to me. I glanced toward the stalls. Elspeth's suitcase was inside the last stall, positioned so nobody could peek under the partition. The lacrosse players flicked water at each other, waved their wet hands in the air and rushed outside.

"Uncle Chuck?" I asked, zipping my pants back up. My voice echoed off the bare concrete.

"Ta da!" said Uncle Chuck, opening the stall door and hanging onto the metal door frame so he could lean out. He was dressed as Elspeth.

I motioned for Elspeth to stay quiet and wait. Then I turned and rushed out the door, checking to see if any other lacrosse players were walking toward us. I checked the baseball diamonds, too.

"It's safe," I yelled, moving away from the door.

Elspeth poked her head outside, looking around. She winked at me and walked to the car. She opened the trunk and put the suitcase inside. She closed the trunk, slung a small bag onto her shoulder and started to walk across the park toward MacArthur Street.

"Uncle Chuck?"

He stopped and turned around.

"Are you sure this is the right thing for you to do?"

He didn't say a word.

"Uncle Chuck," I said, pointing a finger, "you taught me how to misdirect people's attention so you don't have to lie. If you say something like 'Do you think I'd do this if I wasn't sure,' I'll know you're trying to avoid telling a lie, that you aren't sure at all."

"I'm not sure," said Uncle Chuck softly. "I think I'm doing the right thing but, no, I'm not sure."

"Then don't do it," I said, pleading. "Stop. Let's get in the car and go home."

Uncle Chuck took a deep breath. "No," he said, and he turned and walked slowly away from me, humming to himself.

Elspeth didn't have to walk near the hockey rink or the baseball diamond. Nobody looked up. She disappeared into the narrow band of trees that separated the park from MacArthur Street.

I rushed after her.

SEVEN

When I reached the edge of the trees, Elspeth was knocking on the Cluffs' front door.

I didn't think Uncle Chuck would do it.

The door opened. Uncle Chuck said something and opened the screen door himself. He stepped inside, and the screen door gently came to a close behind him. I expected Elspeth to rush from the house, protecting her wig and hiding her head so thrown eggs wouldn't hit her. I expected a slow, quiet drive back home.

I stood up and stretched, then lay behind a tree and stared toward the house, my head rested on folded arms. I waited. My eyes focused on an increasingly smaller area, until I was staring only at the door. Everything around it blurred.

I didn't notice the family until they were standing on the doorstep, getting ready to knock. There were two young children and their parents, dressed in Sunday clothes. The children were carrying flowers. I leaped up and stood behind the tree.

Before they could knock, the front door opened and Elspeth backed onto the crowded porch. Surprised, she looked at the children and pulled a coin from behind the girl's ear.

Elspeth quickly walked down the stairs and turned toward the park. The father stood on the porch, staring after her.

Elspeth walked across the street. The man on the Cluffs' porch kept staring at her. The screen door opened and the man's wife and children stepped inside the house. The father stood on the porch by himself. Somebody inside said something, and the father twisted his head to look. He pretended to check his pockets, keeping Elspeth in sight.

Elspeth was close to me now. "What's happening?" asked Uncle Chuck without turning his head toward me. "Did that man go inside?"

"No," I said. "I think he's going to come after you."

"Geez," said Uncle Chuck. "I know that guy. Ralph Armstrad. He grew up on MacArthur Street, too. I remember him as a boy. He always thought Elspeth was some weirdo, taking advantage of Halloween."

Uncle Chuck started to run. I looked toward the Cluffs' door. Mr. Armstrad was running toward the park.

I could see Uncle Chuck and Mr. Armstrad both, although they couldn't see each other. Uncle Chuck would be caught. He was wearing a dress and carrying a bag full of tricks. Mr. Armstrad was wearing a suit and dress shoes, but he looked like he exercised more than Uncle Chuck. He was younger, too.

I hid in the bushes.

Mr. Armstrad rushed past me.

"Stop, you creep!" he yelled. "I'm going to pound you!"

I didn't think. I sprinted after Mr. Armstrad. He didn't hear me. He was watching Uncle Chuck and getting closer. Mr. Armstrad lifted his arm toward Elspeth just as I leaped at his feet and wrapped my arms around his ankles. He fell to the grass, hard. Being tackled from behind surprised him. It knocked the wind out of Mr. Armstrad and didn't do his suit much good, either.

I leaped up and ran after Uncle Chuck, not looking back. I didn't want Armstrad to see my face. I ran hard and rounded the corner of the washrooms, exhausted. Uncle Chuck was unlocking the car, his wig still in place. A couple of the lacrosse players were staring at us, pointing. A couple of others were staring toward the other side of the washrooms and pointing at something closer to us than the spot where I'd tackled Mr. Armstrad. Mr. Armstrad was coming after us both.

Uncle Chuck unlocked my door. I quickly opened it and slid inside.

"He's coming. Let's go," I yelled.

"What did you do?"

"Go! Go! We don't want him to read the licence plate."

Uncle Chuck backed up the car and then turned toward the park entrance. Low shrubs lined the road into the park. If we could get to the shrubs, Mr. Armstrad wouldn't be able to recognize the car. I stared at the corner of the washrooms, twisting my head as we pulled away. Mr. Armstrad appeared just as we reached the shrubs. He looked tired. He barely glanced at us, knowing we were too far away. His head sank down and he rested his hands on his knees.

"What did you do?" asked Uncle Chuck again.

"I tackled him," I said.

"You what?"

"I tackled him."

"Mr. Armstrad?"

"Yeah."

"He's a big man."

"I'm a big kid," I said, making a muscle.

"No, you're not," said Uncle Chuck. "You're a scrawny kid. You really tackled him?"

"Yeah. He didn't know I was behind him. He wasn't expecting to be tackled. He was expecting to catch you and punch you."

"So, you saved me," said Uncle Chuck, pulling off his wig. He should have kept wearing it. Without the wig, Uncle Chuck looked like a man wearing a dress and lipstick. I looked like the kid riding with him.

"I didn't save you," I said. "I saved Elspeth. If he caught you, he would have torn off your wig and recognized you. He would have told people, too, especially since you went to visit the home of a man who was dying. What happened at the Cluffs?"

Uncle Chuck looked at me, his forehead sweaty. I guess he took off the wig because it was hot.

"We're going to their house later, Max. You'll see."

"Uncle Chuck?"

"Yeah?"

"You'd better change before we get home."

"Good idea. We'll stop someplace and I'll change in the car. I've got walking shorts under the skirt. You really tackled him?"

"Yeah. I tackled him. I did. I wouldn't lie to you, Uncle Chuck."

EIGHT

Denny was in the kitchen when we got home. He glared at us and placed a finger close to his lips. Uncle Chuck waved. It was a small wave, as if a small wave was quieter than a big one. Uncle Chuck tiptoed across the kitchen to the basement door, carrying his suitcase. He looked like a person running away from home in the middle of the night, except he was coming into the house, not leaving. Denny watched him, staring at the suitcase.

"Did we ruin your pies?" I asked.

"Nah. It was all right. But you could have ruined them."

"I live here, too, Denny."

"Meaning what?"

"I don't have to sneak around the place I live."

Denny pointed some sort of kitchen implement at me. I'm not sure what the implement is called or how it's used, although I certainly know most of the standard kitchen utensils.

"And you eat my cooking," he said, tilting his head forward so his eyeballs peered at me over the top of his glasses. It was a threatening glare.

I wasn't sure what he was threatening. Starvation? Poison? I didn't want to suggest options if Denny hadn't considered them. It seemed a good time to change the subject.

"Did you notice what Uncle Chuck was carrying?" I asked.

Denny thought for a moment.

"A suitcase, right?"

"Yeah," I said. "Elspeth's suitcase."

"I thought so," he said. Denny seemed content to know that Uncle Chuck was lugging Elspeth's suitcase into the house without wondering why. My brother is intensely curious about how recipes might taste if one or two spices are replaced by others, but he is not remotely curious about things that bother most people.

"We just came back from the Cluffs' house," I said, wondering if this bit of news might trigger a question, wondering if the fact that we had just returned from the Cluffs' plus the fact that Uncle Chuck was walking around with Elspeth's suitcase might possibly generate The Most Logical Question.

"Aren't we all going there this afternoon?" Denny asked.

It was a question, at least.

The back door opened and Mom walked in. Denny turned and whispered for her to be careful, pointing to the oven like it contained a sleeping baby. A moment later, Uncle Chuck opened the basement door and stepped into the kitchen. Denny swivelled and motioned for him to be quiet, too. Aunt Lois rolled in from the living room. Denny held his finger to his mouth.

None of us moved. The entire family was gathered in the kitchen and none of us said a word. Hobo hopped through her cat door and meandered through the room, taking a moment to stare at each of us like we were nuts.

Aunt Lois snickered and slowly backed her wheelchair into the living room. Uncle Chuck followed her, waving quietly to the rest of us. Mom walked carefully across the room and I followed.

Nobody was in the living room when I got there. They'd all gone off to dress for our visit to the Cluffs'. I looked down at my pants, which were scuffed at the knees, and figured I needed to get cleaned up, too.

When we were all dressed, we looked like an older version of the Armstrad family, decked out in our best clothes. I even wore a tie, mostly because I had seen Mr. Armstrad wearing one. I hoped his tie wasn't ruined.

It was a warm afternoon, so I didn't wear a jacket. My hair was wet and it was combed. I have thin hair that waves around if there is the slightest breeze, so I wore a baseball cap. It was a good cap, though, a purple hat with no sweat stain around the inside of the rim. It was my dress baseball cap, pure cotton with a leather band at the back. There wasn't even a team logo on the front.

Mom wore a dress, which was unusual. Denny wore a tie and a sport coat. Aunt Lois looked fancier than any of us, but she always wore nice dresses, even on the days when she stayed in her study and wrote stories. Uncle Chuck didn't wear a tie at all. He wore a tweed jacket, a nice shirt and jeans. Since Uncle Chuck usually wears a tie all day, he was dressed down, not up.

Uncle Chuck looked at all of us and frowned. I thought he was going to say something like "Oops" and then rush off to change. Instead, he smiled and said, "Let's go. We'll eat later, all right? We'll go out someplace. My treat."

Denny frowned.

"We'll come back here for dessert, though. Those pies sure smell good, Denny."

The pies were out of the oven, sitting on the kitchen table with a couple of dishclothes draped over them. They did smell good.

We all headed for the door. I pushed Aunt Lois. She can push herself, of course, but when we're dressed up it seems more proper that Aunt Lois be pushed. She smiled at me.

I wheeled Aunt Lois down the ramp to the side of Uncle Chuck's car. Uncle Chuck opened the passenger door, and we both helped her inside. I folded the wheelchair, slid it into the trunk and then crawled into the back seat. Mom sat beside me and Denny sat beside her. Uncle Chuck drove down the street. We stopped at the corner light and drove for a while in silence.

"You know," said Uncle Chuck, as we pulled onto MacArthur Street, "Mr. Cluff is not going to look too healthy. He's thin. He doesn't have much hair, and he doesn't have much energy, either."

"We know," said Denny. "We're not stupid."

"No," said Uncle Chuck. "But there's something else I should tell all of you."

"Now?" asked Mom.

"Now," said Uncle Chuck.

"Before we see the Cluffs?"

"Well, it's about the Cluffs."

"What is it?" asked Aunt Lois.

"I saw Mr. Cluff earlier this afternoon."

I saw Mom frown. I glanced at Aunt Lois. She was frowning, too. They didn't understand.

"Where was he?" asked Denny, confused.

"In his house," said Uncle Chuck.

"You went to see him even though you knew we'd be visiting now?" asked Aunt Lois.

"Why?" asked Mom.

I glanced at Denny. He was thinking, trying to remember what I'd said in the kitchen.

"Oh, no," said Denny loudly. "You didn't. Tell me you didn't, Uncle Chuck!"

"Didn't what?" asked Mom. Denny leaned across Mom and looked at me.

"He didn't?" he asked. "Did he?"

"He did," I said, trying to make it obvious that I wished he hadn't.

"Did what?" asked Mom and Aunt Lois together.

"Uncle Chuck dressed up like Elspeth this afternoon and went to visit Mr. Cluff," said Denny.

Aunt Lois turned in her seat and stared at Uncle Chuck. Uncle Chuck didn't say anything. He adjusted the rear-view mirror.

"Oh, no," groaned Aunt Lois. "It's true."

"We're here," said Uncle Chuck, pulling to the curb. "Don't give me away when we go inside."

"I don't think I can go," said Denny. "I mean, I've never talked to somebody who is dying. And now that Uncle Chuck did what he did, I can't. I just can't. I'll wait in the car."

"You are not waiting in the car," snapped Mom, turning toward Denny. "You are going inside with the rest of us. And believe me," she added, anger in her voice as she leaned into the gap between the two front seats so she couldn't be ignored, "we don't want anyone to find out that Elspeth is related to us. We won't tell."

"Why would you do such a stupid thing, Chuck?" added Aunt Lois quietly.

"I hope," said Uncle Chuck, "that it wasn't such a stupid thing."

Mom muttered something to herself. I helped Aunt Lois out of the car and into her wheelchair. She refused to let Uncle Chuck help. He stood on the sidewalk and tried not to look at any of us. We walked along the path and up to the Cluffs' front porch.

I helped Aunt Lois out of her wheelchair near the bottom step.

Mom rang the doorbell. Mrs. Cluff moved a curtain and peeked out the front window. She waved. We didn't wave back. We each stood still. Mrs. Cluff turned to the room behind her, said something and let the curtain go. A few seconds later, we could hear her unlock the door.

NINE

"Come inside," said Mrs. Cluff. "I thought I saw all of you walking up. My, Denny, you've grown. It's been what, a year?"

Denny nodded. He didn't go to MacArthur Street on Halloween anymore, but he had seen the Cluffs at a picnic.

"This is for you," Denny said, holding out a pie.

I hadn't noticed the pie, even in the car.

"Did you make it?" asked Mrs. Cluff.

Denny nodded.

"Thank you," she said, giving him a hug. Then she looked at me over Denny's shoulder.

"I didn't bring anything," I said apologetically.

She smiled and hugged me while Uncle Chuck and Denny helped Aunt Lois into the living room.

"We have more food than we could eat in a year," she whispered. "We don't need food. We just need friends. Come inside."

Mrs. Cluff took me by the hand and led me into the living room. Mom and Aunt Lois and Uncle Chuck were already sitting in chairs, facing Mr. Cluff.

He sat on a small couch, looking straight at me.

If it wasn't for the eyes, I would have thought he was dead already. He was wearing a shirt and tie but the collar was so loose, his neck looked like a turtle's, sticking out from its shell. He looked like a skeleton with flesh loosely hanging from the bones. I must have reacted because Mrs. Cluff squeezed my hand and led me forward.

"You remember Max Junior, don't you, Tim," she said.

He smiled at me and carefully reached up to shake my hand.

I held out my free hand. Mr. Cluff, who had helped my grandfather lay a brick patio when my grandparents lived next door, placed his bony hand inside mine and left it there, limp. I rubbed more than shook it and smiled weakly at him. His skin was a sickly yellow shade. Two tiny tubes rested under his nose, connected to a bottle of clear liquid beside his chair. I looked around the room, wanting to sit down. The chairs were taken so I had to sit beside Mr. Cluff on the couch.

"You look good," Mom said to Mr. Cluff unconvincingly. I recognized her comment as a noble lie and glanced at Uncle Chuck, wondering what he would say.

"You must be glad to be home, Tim," said Uncle Chuck.

Mr. Cluff grinned and nodded. Aunt Lois was smiling. Denny was looking toward the front window. His legs were bouncing nervously.

"Guess who came to visit me this afternoon," said Mr. Cluff slowly, mostly to me, since I was the closest. Everyone could hear him, though. There was no other sound in the room. No stereo. No television.

We all leaned forward to listen so he didn't have to talk loudly.

I could have answered Mr. Cluff's question, but I didn't. I shrugged.

"Elspeth," said Mr. Cluff. "Do you remember Elspeth?"

"That clown who comes around on Halloween nights?" asked Mom. She emphasized the word "clown," looking at Uncle Chuck but trying to make it a casual look which he would understand without having its meaning telegraphed to the Cluffs.

Mr. Cluff slowly turned and looked at Mom. He smiled. "Yes," he said in a whisper.

"I've always been fond of her," said Uncle Chuck, grinning innocently. "She was wonderful."

"She still is wonderful," said Mrs. Cluff, talking so her husband could rest. Mrs. Cluff is big. Not huge and not fat — just big. She's tall and wide and thick and looks like she's been big all her life. She also has the fastest, busiest eyes I've ever seen. They sweep a room in a random pattern, like spotlights, missing nothing.

"It was so odd to see her this afternoon," she said. "There was a knock. I went to the door, opened it, and there stood Elspeth. I was so shocked. I mean, Elspeth has never appeared except on Halloween night. Not that I know of. Have any of you ever heard of Elspeth going to somebody's house except on Halloween?"

"No," said Uncle Chuck. "I'm sure it's a first. What did she say?"

"Well," said Mrs. Cluff, "she said that she'd heard Tim was sick so she came to see him. I didn't want to let her inside the house. It just didn't seem right. I mumbled something about Tim being in the bathroom, which was true, and Elspeth walked right past me and headed down the hall. She marched straight to the bathroom door, swung it open and shouted, 'Ah, Mr. Cluff. There you are. I heard you were sick so I came right over to make you feel better.'"

"She walked right into the bathroom?" asked Denny slowly.

"Yes," said Mrs. Cluff.

"Where . . . uh . . . where was . . . "

"I was sitting on the toilet," said Mr. Cluff. "She draped a towel over my lap, and do you know what she said?"

He waited for us to guess.

"What?" I asked.

"'Pick a card.' Elspeth spread a deck of cards on the towel and said, 'Pick a card.'"

I looked at Aunt Lois and saw her glare at Uncle Chuck. He seemed to be inspecting the carpet. Mom sighed and rubbed her head with her fingertips.

"I'll cut the pie," said Denny, standing up. "Who wants some? It's strawberry rhubarb."

Uncle Chuck smiled and raised his hand. "I'll have a piece," he said. Nobody else raised a hand. Denny waited a moment and then picked up the pie from the coffee table and raced to the kitchen.

"I picked the four of clubs," said Mr. Cluff proudly. "And then I slid it back into the deck and Elspeth shuffled the cards, held them in her palm, and we both watched as the four of clubs rose out of the deck all by itself."

"I saw it, too," said Mrs. Cluff. "I was standing at the door and the four of clubs just rose up. Elspeth pulled it out of the air and started to hand it to me. When I reached for the card, it disappeared and Elspeth was holding a red rose. Look, I put the rose in a vase on top of the piano."

We all looked at the rose.

"What happened next?" I asked Mr. Cluff.

"You should have been here, Max. I never realized Elspeth was so good. I mean, she performs for kids, right? Besides, I don't like magicians. They are so corny. But I sat on the toilet and Elspeth made sponge balls disappear from my hand when they were supposed to be in her hand. She juggled. She did coin tricks and scarf tricks and rope tricks, all for me."

Mr. Cluff stopped. He was breathing heavily. He reached beside him and picked up a plastic oxygen mask. He held the mask close to his face and then put it back down.

"Elspeth was great," he said slowly.

"What a surprise. I'm sitting on the john and suddenly the door swings open and Elspeth is standing there. I didn't recognize her at first, of course. It looked like some strange woman. 'Pick a card,' she said. I swear that's what happened. 'Pick a card,' like it was the most natural thing in the world for one person to say to another after barging into the bathroom."

The kitchen door opened. Denny walked toward Uncle Chuck and handed him the smallest slice of pie I'd ever seen.

"Mrs. Cluff," said Denny, turning around. "It's getting close to dinner time so I'm warming up one of the casseroles somebody brought. I'm going to add a few herbs, though. Is that all right?"

"Certainly," said Mrs. Cluff.

Denny raced back to the kitchen, happy to be doing something helpful and to be missing the visit. Nobody said anything for a moment.

"How's the bridge coming, Tim?" asked Mom at last.

"It's finished," said Mr. Cluff.

"Really?" said Mom. "That's terrific. I'm surprised, though. You still had a lot of work to do, didn't you?"

"Yes, I did."

"Can we see it?" she asked, like she did each Halloween night.

"Yes," said Mr. Cluff, nodding slightly. "You can see my bridge."

Mom looked shocked.

"We can? Did an artist draw it for you or something?"

"No," said Mr. Cluff in a whisper. "A drawing wouldn't be my bridge. An artist can draw a bridge spanning the distance between two clouds and make it appear solid and firm." Mr. Cluff leaned forward and patted the arm of the couch with his tiny closed fist. "My bridge is a real bridge," he said, excitement in his eyes even though his voice was weak. "My bridge isn't some creature of the imagination."

"I don't understand," I said. "It's in your head, right?"

"Tell them, Ida," said Mr. Cluff. "Tell them."

He slumped back and breathed deeply.

"It's a real bridge," said Mrs. Cluff calmly. "I've seen it. It can stand up to 600 kilometre an hour winds and can be built under budget. It contains some unique engineering concepts that may be used in the construction of other real bridges."

I figured Mrs. Cluff was telling a noble lie.

"Great," I said, trying to smile. Mom and Aunt Lois tried to smile, too, so they must have decided the same thing.

"It happened in the hospital," said Mrs. Cluff. "I was telling one of the nurses about the bridge. The nurse, Caleb, has a girlfriend who is a graduate civil engineering student, and I guess he told her about this bridge Tim has been building in his head. Caleb's girlfriend, Samantha, came to see Tim, and he told her about the bridge, too. Anyway, Samantha came every day, ten days in a row. She asked about building materials and design features and construction methods. She collected all Tim's soil calculations and figures."

"I had every fact, every figure she needed," said Mr. Cluff quietly. "Everything. All in my head."

His wife nodded and kept talking.

"Samantha put all these figures into a computer program that tests bridge designs. The program shows you a picture of the bridge, and it tells the designer what the bridge will do if the wind blows hard or if there's an earthquake. It even evaluates the materials and the site and produces a cost of construction. After Tim gave Sam all those figures, I sort of forgot about her.

"Then a week ago I was sitting beside Tim's bed, holding his hand, when Samantha walks into the room carrying a little case. It looked like a backgammon set, but it was a computer, one of those small notebook computers.

"Samantha didn't say a word. She set the computer on that table patients use for meals, and she plugged the computer into the back of a big monitor and plugged both machines into a wall socket."

"She asked if I wanted to see my bridge," said Mr. Cluff, "and I said I did."

"She turned on the computer," said Mrs. Cluff. "I never did like those things. Too impersonal, I thought. But there was Tim's bridge. I thought we'd see a picture, but there was the bridge and by moving this little control, Tim could fly around it and under it and drive through it and look at it from any angle he wanted."

"It's beautiful," said Mr. Cluff softly. "And at each end of the bridge there is bronze plaque that says, 'The Ida Cluff Bridge, designed by Tim Cluff.'"

He reached for the oxygen again and put it

down. "Samantha put my bridge through a hurricane and a tornado and a monsoon and it barely swayed. I built it, and I built it well."

"Can we see it?" asked Mom.

"Sure," said Mr. Cluff. "We don't have a computer or anything, but . . . "

"I have one," said Aunt Lois softly. "Have Samantha make me a copy of the program. I'd like to keep it."

Mr. Cluff nodded.

"You can come see it any time you want, Ida," said Aunt Lois.

Mrs. Cluff shook her head. "The bridge is in my head, now, too," she said. "I think that's a good place for it. Seeing that bridge was the most exciting thing that has ever happened to me."

Mrs. Cluff looked at her husband and smiled. It was a broad, gorgeous smile. I could tell that she thought this withered, dying man was the most handsome and attactive man she had ever seen, and she loved him.

"But it was also bizarre," said Mrs. Cluff, glancing around the room at each of us. "It was like I was staring inside Tim's head. I loved seeing Tim's bridge, but I don't need to see it again."

"'Pick a card,'" said Mr. Cluff. "Elspeth came right into the bathroom while I was sitting on the toilet. She put a towel across my lap, spread out a deck of cards and told me to pick a card. I'm going to tell everybody. Scared me silly, she did. I thought she was some strange woman at first, not Elspeth."

"We should go now," said Aunt Lois.

"You're probably right," said Mrs. Cluff, smiling gently. "Tim is tired. He needs a nap."

"Goodbye," said Mr. Cluff, smiling weakly. "Geez, you should have seen Elspeth. It was something to remember."

Mrs. Cluff walked us to the door and gave us each a hug.

"Thanks for coming," she said.

She hugged Uncle Chuck last and longest.

"Thank you," she said, holding onto his shoulders and staring at him. "Thank you so much."

"You're welcome," said Uncle Chuck. "We're glad for the chance to visit. Tim is a terrific man. It's wonderful, his bridge being finished."

"Yes," said Mrs. Cluff. "It is wonderful. But you know, I have never been so scared as when Samantha turned on that computer and showed us The Ida Cluff Bridge, complete with plaque. Tim has been working on that bridge ever since we got married. Working on the bridge was part of our life. I hated to see it finished, even though I would have hated it even more if Tim had died without finishing his bridge. You know?"

Mom nodded.

"Of course you know," said Mrs. Cluff, opening the door. "I forgot, just for a moment. I think of Max, your husband, all the time. To me, he is frozen in time as the little boy next door."

"And to me," said Mom, squeezing Mrs. Cluff's hand, "he will always be a man half asleep, wearing his bathrobe, sitting in a rocking chair while holding one of our babies."

"The Armstrads were here this afternoon," said Mrs. Cluff calmly, looking straight at Uncle Chuck. "They arrived just as Elspeth was leaving. Mr. Armstrad said he had to go back to the car for something, but I watched him run toward the park. I don't know what happened, but when he came back the knees were torn out of his suit. He didn't look too happy, so I guess he didn't catch Elspeth. If I were her, I'd be careful next Halloween."

TEN

We pulled away from the curb.

"What happened?" asked Denny, who could tell he'd missed something.

"Well, I'd say that Elspeth got caught," said Uncle Chuck. He turned to Aunt Lois. "Didn't you feel that Ida was trying to tell us that she recognized me?"

"It wasn't too subtle," said Mom. "Yes, she recognized you. I guess Elspeth's disguise is better at night."

"So, she knows I'm Elspeth."

"Yes," said Mom. "She knows."

"Then it's a good thing they didn't mind," said Uncle Chuck. "Now that it's over, I'll admit that I was a bit nervous. I mean, I was sure everything would work out, but my plan . . . "

"What was the plan?" asked Aunt Lois, glaring at Uncle Chuck. "I know Mr. Cluff enjoyed Elspeth's visit, but it still seems a risky, stupid thing to do. It was crazy."

"Just a moment," said Uncle Chuck. "I've

got to make a call."

He reached down and picked up the phone, punching numbers while keeping an eye on the road.

"Hello," he said. "Is this Phil's Restaurant? There are five of us. Do you have a table? We're only a few blocks away. What? Non-smoking. Good. Thanks. We'll be there in a few minutes. The name? Put the reservation under the name Porchsenhoser." Uncle Chuck winked at me in the rear-view mirror so I'd know he hadn't told a lie. He'd never said our name was Porchsenhoser.

Uncle Chuck hung up and placed the phone back into its cradle.

"Phone calls and funny names aren't going to make us forget," said Aunt Lois. "Why did you do it, Chuck? What if Mr. Cluff had hated the fact that a clown came to visit?"

"I know Mr. Cluff better than anybody in this car," said Uncle Chuck. "He was my father's best friend. I grew up with Mr. Cluff."

The car pulled into Phil's parking lot and swung into a space.

"But you couldn't have been sure," said Aunt Lois. "You could have offended those people. You could have made them miserable."

Uncle Chuck turned off the engine and

pulled the parking brake. He didn't unbuckle his seatbelt, and neither did we. We all sat still, staring through the front windshield at the side of the restaurant.

"Elspeth visited Mr. Cluff this afternoon because of Max, my brother," said Uncle Chuck. "The day Max was admitted to the hospital for the last time, I stayed all day. Do you remember, Marta?"

"Yes, of course. I was there."

"We knew he was dying. He knew he was dying, too."

Mom nodded, which Uncle Chuck couldn't see because he was still staring at the restaurant wall. He seemed to know that she had nodded, though.

"The three of us talked about the past. You and Max talked about your honeymoon and your children. He and I talked about things that had happened when we were kids. Do you remember, Marta?"

"Yes," she said softly.

"We were trying to justify that Max had lived a life worth living, a life filled with wonderful moments spent with people who loved him. After a couple of hours, during which we did absolutely nothing but talk about the past, Max looked at us and said, 'We've got to stop. It's like my entire life is past tense. But I'm still alive. New things happen every day, and I see them and they become part of my life.' He said that, or something close. Do you remember?"

"I remember," said Mom.

"He was right, you know."

"I know," said Mom.

"Every day, after that first day, you told Max exactly what Max Junior said at breakfast or what happened at Denny's T-ball game. If Denny missed the ball every time, that's what you told Max, because that's what happened and Max loved Denny and wanted to know. You never pretended everything was fine because life is story and story is drama and drama is unpredictable. You never lied, and it was the right thing to do. I have never lied since the day my brother died.

"Max taught me that life is not life unless there are new stories to tell. We all need to know that something unusual might happen today or tomorrow, something we can tell people.

"So," said Uncle Chuck after a moment, "when I heard that Mr. Cluff was coming home from the hospital and that everyone would be stopping by to see him, I knew all his friends would want to talk about the past. I figured Mr. Cluff needed a story to tell, something new, something that had just happened to him. Max Junior gave me the idea," said Uncle Chuck, pointing a thumb at me. "He said I should tell Mr. Cluff I was Elspeth. And I knew that if Elspeth knocked on the door, Elspeth who never appeared anywhere except on Halloween night, then it would be a story. So, that's what Elspeth did. She made her one and only appearance on a night other than Halloween."

A car pulled into the spot next to us and a family hopped out. I could see the mother glance into our car. There we sat, a silent family of five. Aunt Lois was crying. Denny, too.

"Good for Elspeth," said Mom at last. "I'm proud of her."

"I have never liked Elspeth," said Aunt Lois. "I hated the fact that you went back to MacArthur Street every year. I don't know why, but it always seemed silly for a grown man to dress up like a clown once a year, keeping this strange person a secret from everyone."

Aunt Lois paused for a moment and then added, "I've never gone to see Elspeth, you know. But I'll go next year. I think I could enjoy her now."

"Is there going to be a next year?" asked Mom.

"What do you mean?" asked Uncle Chuck.

"Mr. Armstrad," said Mom. "His suit is wrecked and he seems to blame Elspeth. Don't you think he'll be waiting for her?"

"We'll work it out," said Uncle Chuck. "Come on. Let's go. They won't hold that table forever."

We climbed out of the car. I helped Aunt Lois while Denny pulled her wheelchair out of the trunk and flipped it open.

"I'm ready," said Mom, taking Denny's arm while I pushed Aunt Lois.

"Go ahead," said Uncle Chuck. "I'll be there in a minute."

"Oh, Chuck," said Aunt Lois. "Another call? Can't it wait?"

"I won't be long," he said. "Promise."

I pushed Aunt Lois down the walkway. Just before we turned into the restaurant, I peeked back at the car. Uncle Chuck sat in the car, gazing out the window. There was no phone in his hand.

ELEVEN

It was Halloween night. Elspeth's crowd waited at the top of MacArthur Street. Flashlight beams occasionally drifted into the park itself, searching for her. Everyone seemed to know that they had to wait for Elspeth behind the log. It wouldn't be right to go and look for her. It might ruin the spell. She had to emerge from the trees as if there were no ball diamond behind her.

Mrs. Cluff waited with the crowd, not at her house. She had asked Mr. Armstrad to wait with her.

Waiting for Elspeth was like waiting for a fish to bite. It was an uncertain waiting. Elspeth had always come before, but there was no guarantee she would come again.

Aunt Lois waited with Mrs. Cluff and Mr. Armstrad. Her wheelchair was decorated for the evening, crepe paper woven through the wheels and a playing card attached to each rim so the wheels made noise when the chair rolled.

Mom and Denny waited, too. Mom was dressed like a fairy, complete with gossamer wings and a tinfoil wand with a star at the end. Denny was dressed like a chef, with a tall hat, a white coat and a phony black moustache.

"There she is!" shouted a young dinosaur. "There she is!"

People looked at the dinosaur to see where her paw was pointed and then aimed their flashlights in the same direction.

Elspeth was walking across the grass, but she wasn't alone. Another clown walked beside her. The second clown was shorter than Elspeth. He had a red nose and bright yellow yarn hair. He wore baggy men's pants and a green shirt with a long, multi-coloured tie.

I was the smaller clown, and I was nervous.

I stepped over the log first and held out my arm to help Elspeth. The crowd cheered, which made me feel better. Elspeth bowed, but I didn't. They were cheering for Elspeth because she had come again. They didn't know me.

I drew a chalk line in a semi-circle on the street, creating space for us to perform.

Elspeth dropped her bag and pulled out three oranges. She began to juggle, pretending to reach for each orange as it almost fell to the ground.

She stopped and bowed again. The crowd cheered.

Elspeth tossed the oranges to me, one at a time. I caught them.

"My assistant," said Elspeth. "His name is Timmy."

I waved to the crowd. They clapped politely.

Elspeth reached into her bag and produced three more balls. We had practised our trick together many times in the basement and then in Mr. Singh's backyard. We juggled at the same time and in the same rhythm. It isn't hard, once you learn.

Slowly, we turned toward each other and began to toss oranges back and forth, every third at first and then every other orange and finally every orange, creating a flurry.

Elspeth turned and bowed. I kept tossing the oranges, sending them over Elspeth's head and into the park while pretending that I thought I was still getting oranges and tossing them back.

The crowd laughed.

I looked mystified, as we had planned, wondering where the oranges had gone. I scratched my head, shrugged and then took a bow.

I spotted Mom, Aunt Lois and Denny. Mr. Armstrad stood beside Denny, staring at me, knowing I was the one who had tackled him.

I walked over to him, pulled a flower from behind his ear and handed it to him. He took the flower from me and smiled ever so slightly. I smiled back.

Behind the crowd, on the sidewalk on the other side of the street, I saw Mrs. Cluff walking home so she'd be there when we arrived. Hurry, I thought, we'll be there soon to do some tricks. This year, though, I won't be returning for hot chocolate after the last trick. I'll be riding away in the back of Mr. Singh's taxi, with Elspeth.

OTHER BOOKS BY KEN ROBERTS

Crazy Ideas

Jon and Christine Anastasiou live in Sceletown, where the streets are laid out like a skeleton so that citizens can learn anatomy. They need a crazy idea to graduate from Max Barca Junior High School. That's no problem for Jon — he's crazy enough to invent the fourth most popular comic book in Canada. But Christine is having trouble. She can't seem to think of anything nutty but workable. Until one day, hanging out in Mandible Park, she sees a wrecking crew demolishing the Endicott Hotel, and her crazy idea begins to grow.

ISBN 0-88899-131-2 $6.95

Pop Bottles

Will McCleary lives in Vancouver in 1933. Times are difficult, and everyone is dealing with the Depression in their own ways. Will's father sits in his rocking chair and stares dreamily at the mountains; Will's mother, a nomad at heart, likes to move house a lot. Will spends his time hanging out with his best friend, Ray, and practising his bolo-bat technique.

It looks as if it will be a fairly uneventful summer ...until the day Will discovers that the walkway in front of his new house is made from thousands of pop bottles, buried in the ground so that only the round bottoms show. Each bottle is worth two cents at the local store, and Will knows that he has found buried treasure.

ISBN 0-88899-059-6 $5.95

Hiccup Champion of the World

Maynard Chan is a normal twelve-year-old boy. He has friends. He gets above-average marks in school. Then one day Maynard gets the hiccups, which seems pretty normal, too — at first.

Three months later Maynard is still hiccuping, and he's getting tired of being a guinea pig, as neighbours, relatives and classmates try out their favourite hiccup cures — from Mr. Tanaka (the retired sumo wrestler) helpfully offering to squeeze the hiccups out of him, to creepy little Susie, who innocently suggests to Maynard's mother that eating two bowls of cold oatmeal is a sure-fire cure.

ISBN 0-88899-071-5 $5.95

Nothing Wright

Sam Wright's brother, Noel, has the worst luck in the world. When something bad happens to him, it keeps on happening over and over again. No one can explain it or make it go away. Things have become so bad that Noel has a nickname — Nothing Wright.

Then Emma Shipworth, the most obnoxious girl in the school, decides to get to the bottom of Noel's problem. Will she be able to change his life? Or is she just another piece of bad luck?

ISBN 0-88899-137-1 $6.95